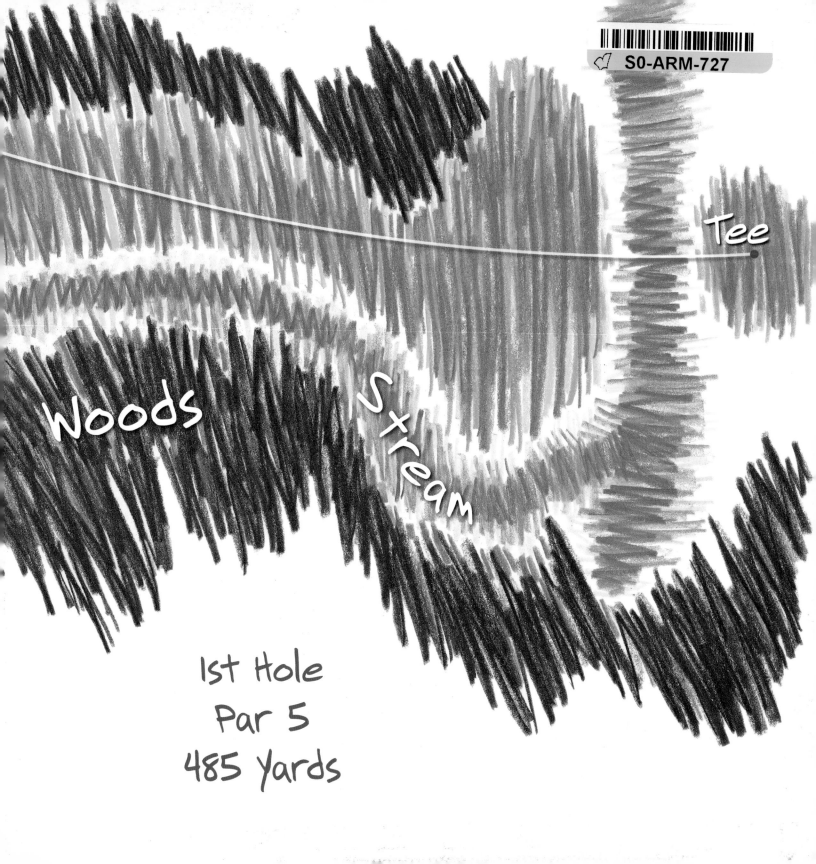

Tee

Woods

Stream

1st Hole
Par 5
485 Yards

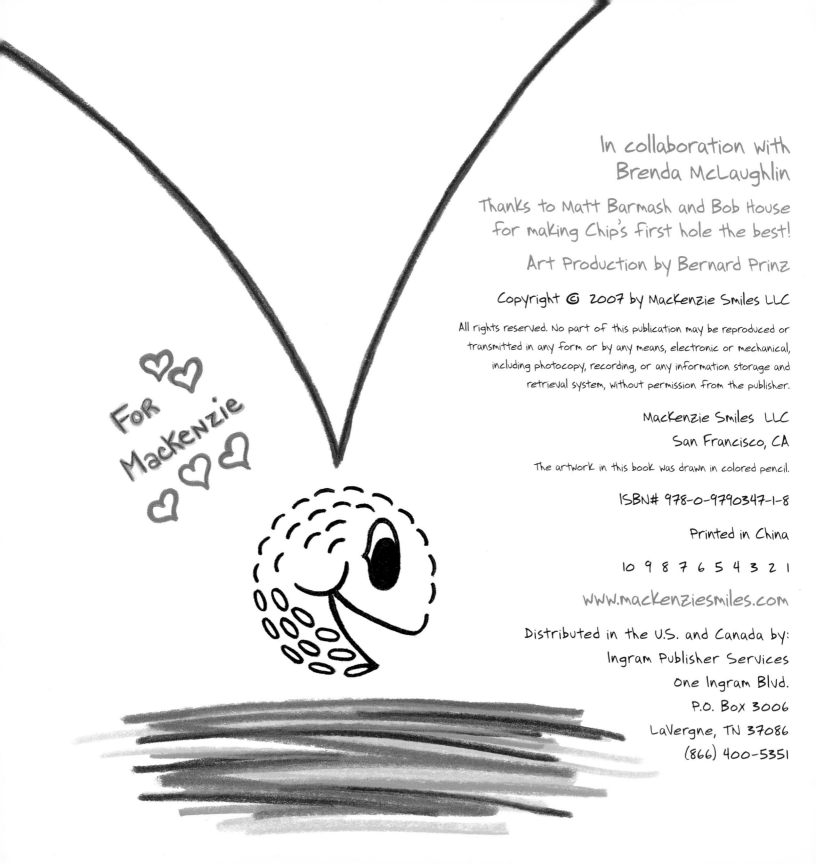

For Mackenzie

In collaboration with
Brenda McLaughlin

Thanks to Matt Barmash and Bob House
for making Chip's first hole the best!

Art Production by Bernard Prinz

MacKenzie Smiles LLC
San Francisco, CA

The artwork in this book was drawn in colored pencil.

ISBN# 978-0-9790347-1-8

Printed in China

10 9 8 7 6 5 4 3 2 1

www.mackenziesmiles.com

Distributed in the U.S. and Canada by:
Ingram Publisher Services
One Ingram Blvd.
P.O. Box 3006
LaVergne, TN 37086
(866) 400-5351

What a beautiful day for the
rookie balls back from golf camp.
This should be a fun round to watch.

Chip is very excited. It's his first day on the golf course. He's been practicing balancing on the tee all week. He's ready to tee off!

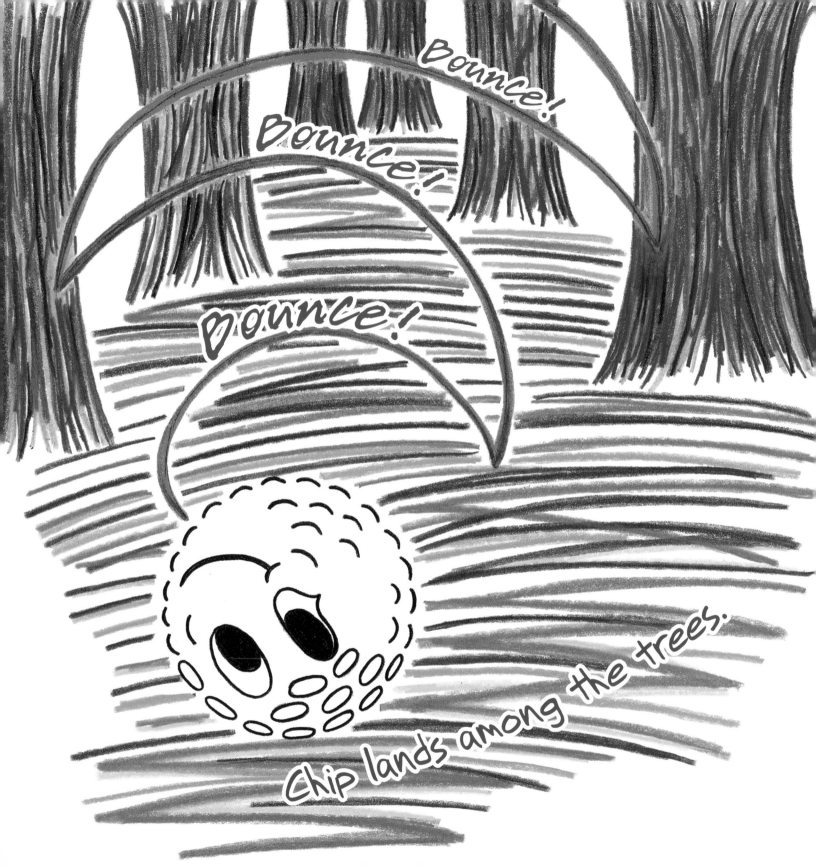

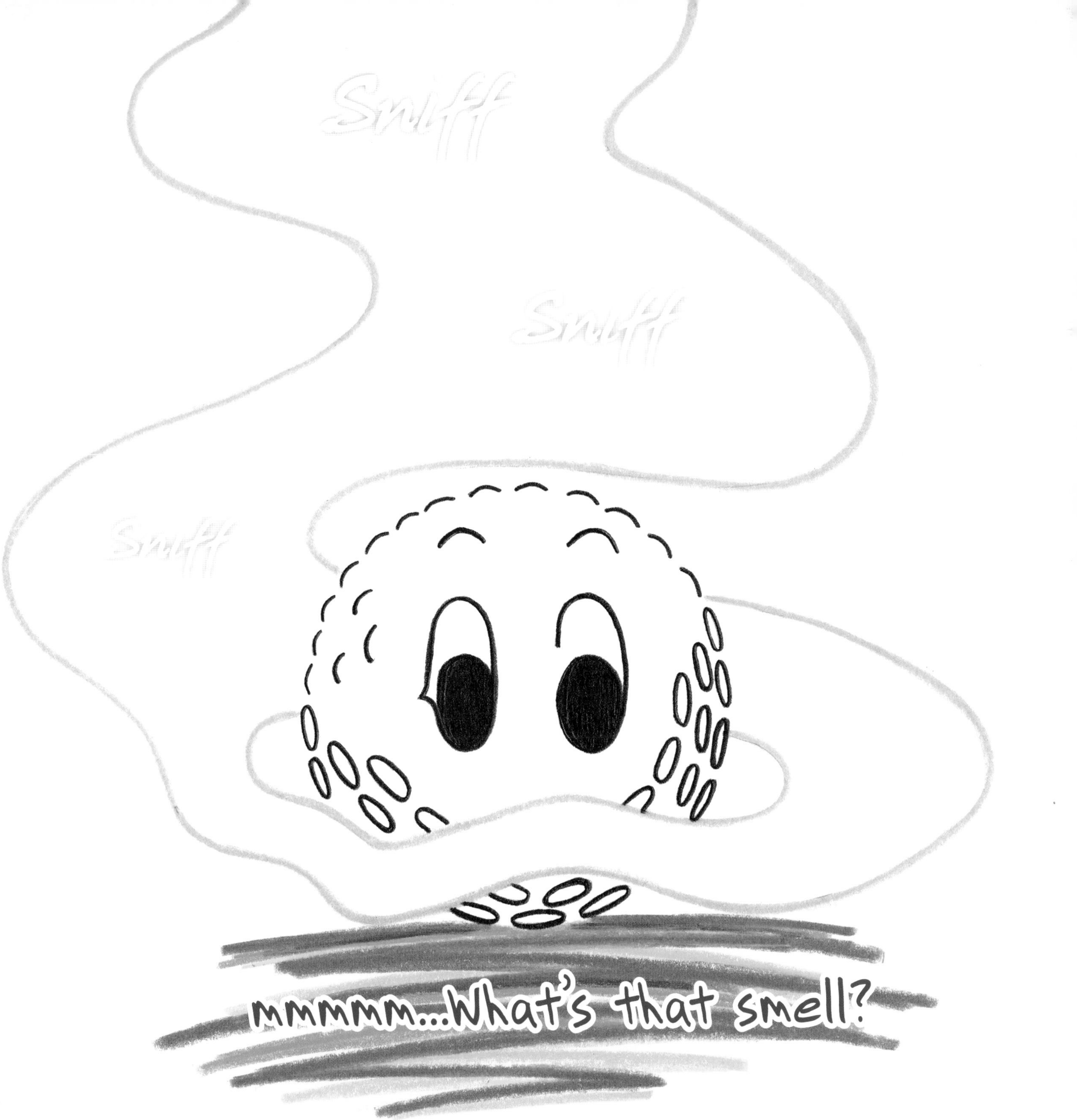
Sniff
Sniff
Sniff
mmmmm...What's that smell?

...Marshmallows!

"Hi Divot! Hi Sandy! Hi Wedge!" says Chip.
"How long have you been here?"
"Since yesterday. Divot's battery is dead
so we couldn't call for help," replies Sandy.

"Thank you
Rescue Squirrel!" yells Chip,
"I hope my second
shot's better."

THWACK!

Chip soars through the air.

UP! UP! UP!

He loves the wind in his face.

Looks like a 3-wood with about 220 yards to the green.

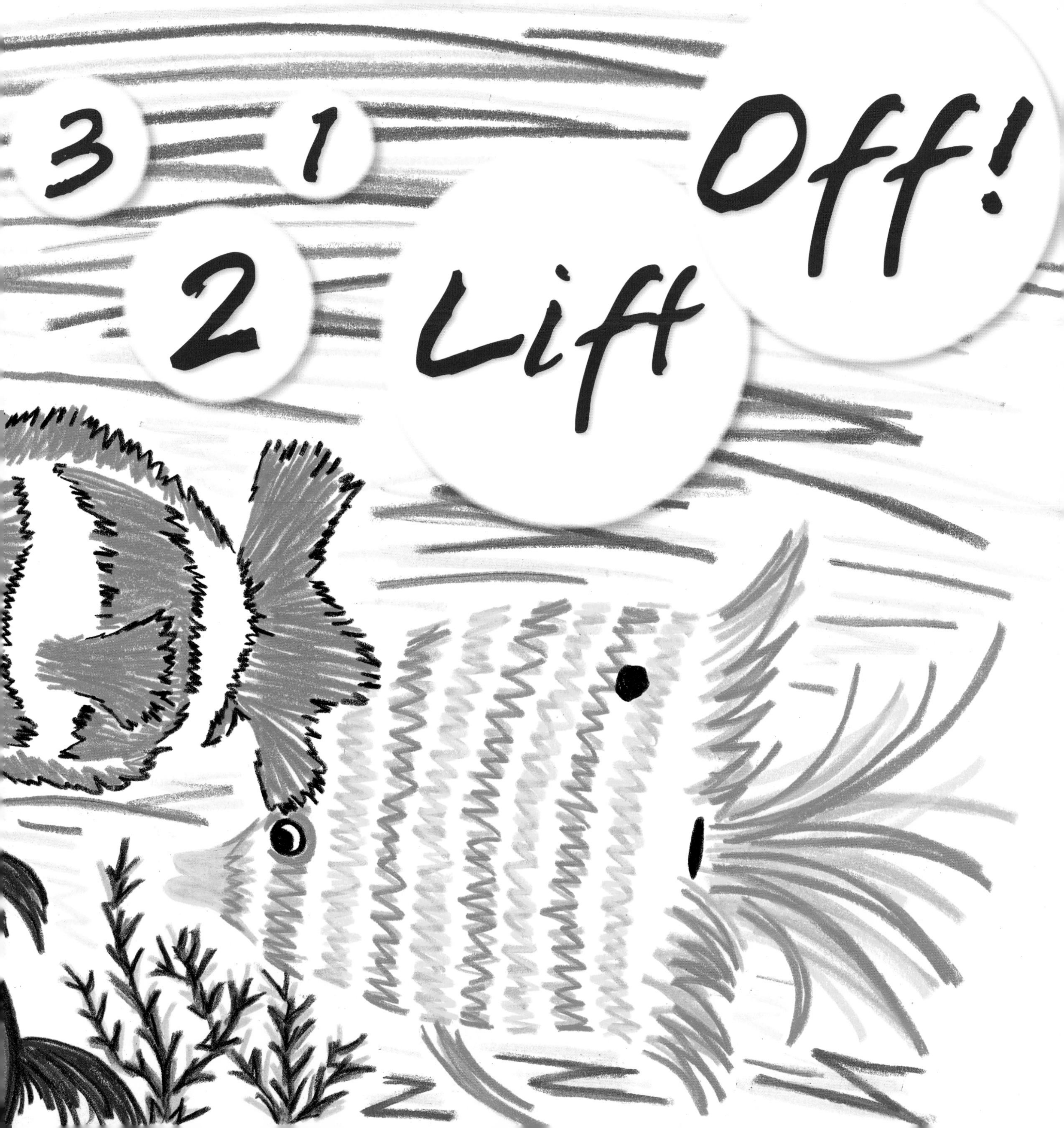
3
2
1
Lift
Off!

Chip zooms through the water and into the air.

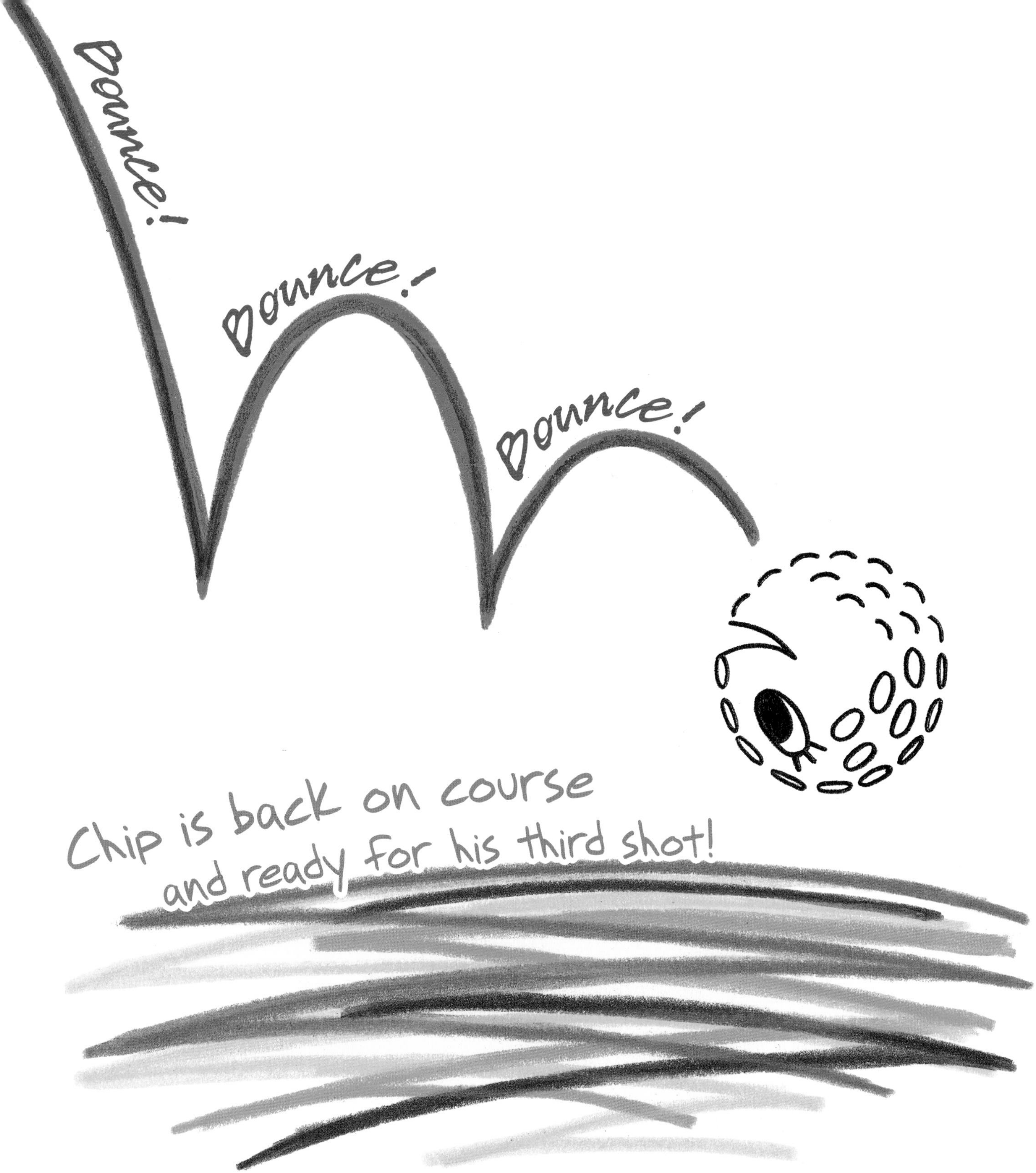

Chip is back on course
and ready for his third shot!

SMACK!

UP! UP! **UP!**

Chip can see the whole course.

OH, NO!

He's headed for the sand trap!

A 9-iron?
Should have used a pitching wedge
with only 90 yards to the hole.

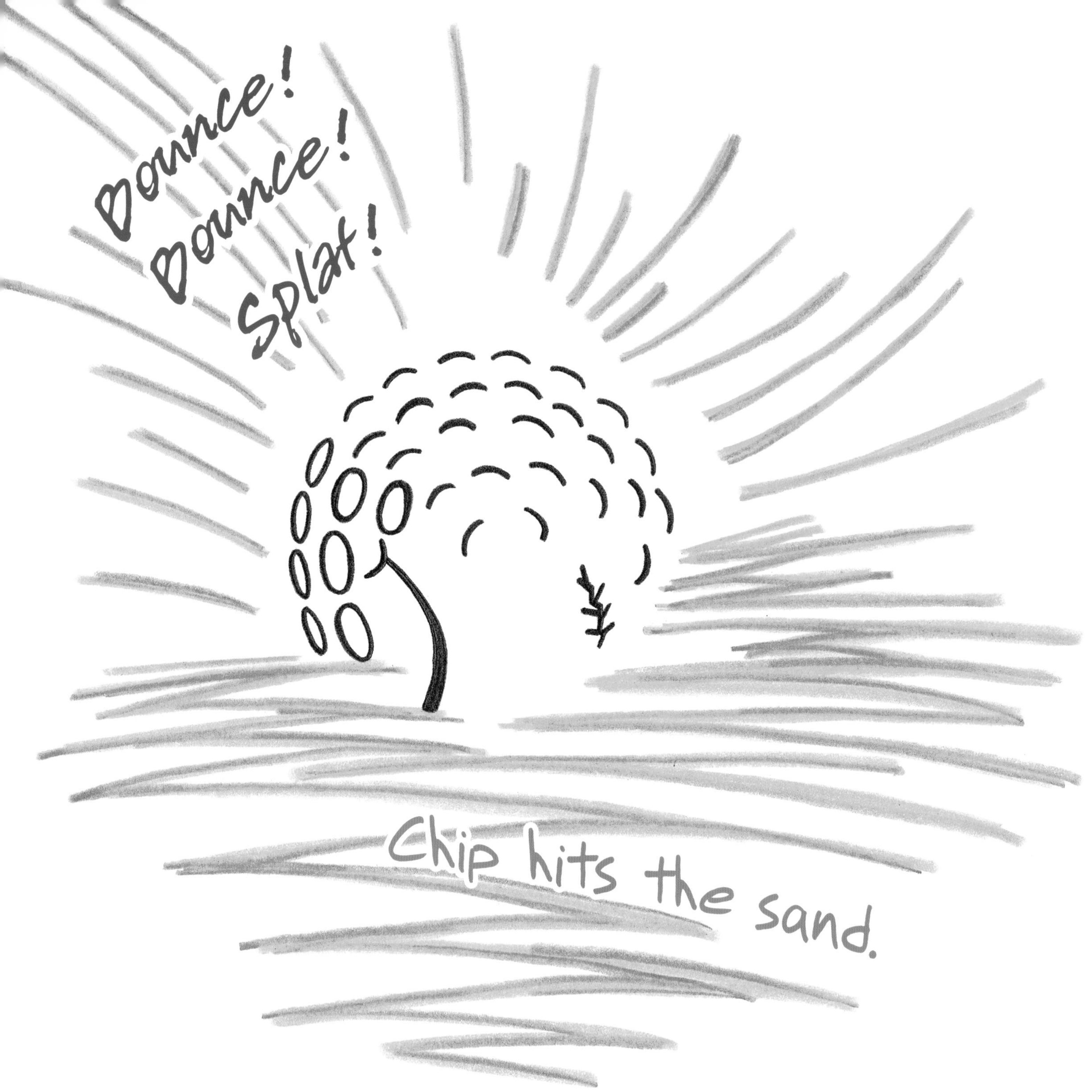

Chip hits the sand.

"Wow, this is just like the beach," giggles Chip.

"Let's get a move on," urges the Marshal. "There's a foursome waiting behind you."

"Sorry," apologizes Chip.

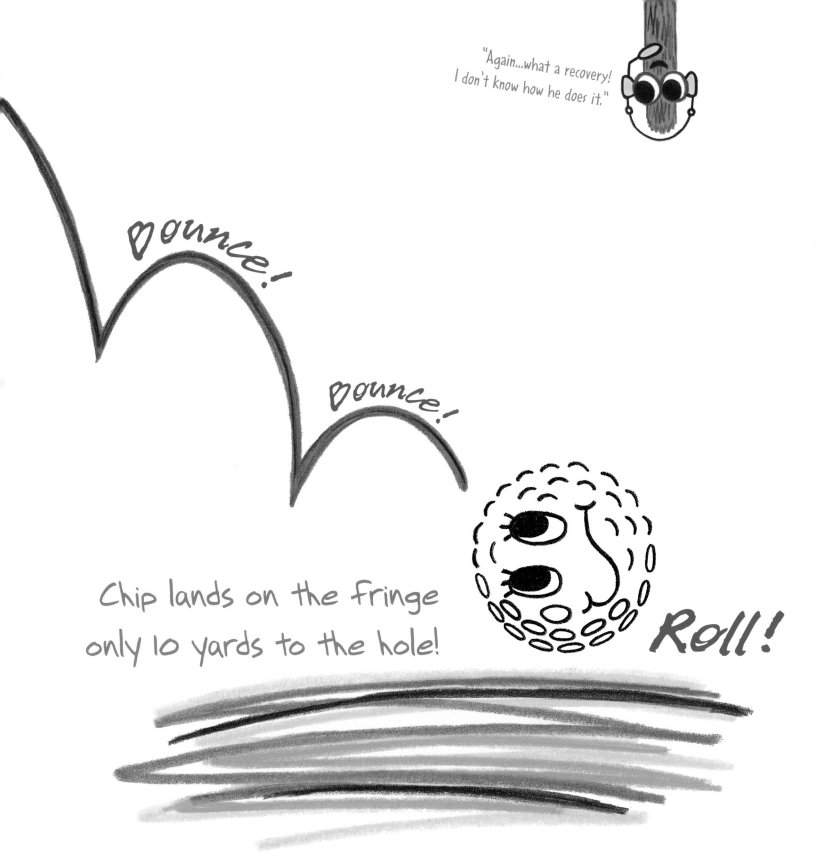

Chip's just above the pin.

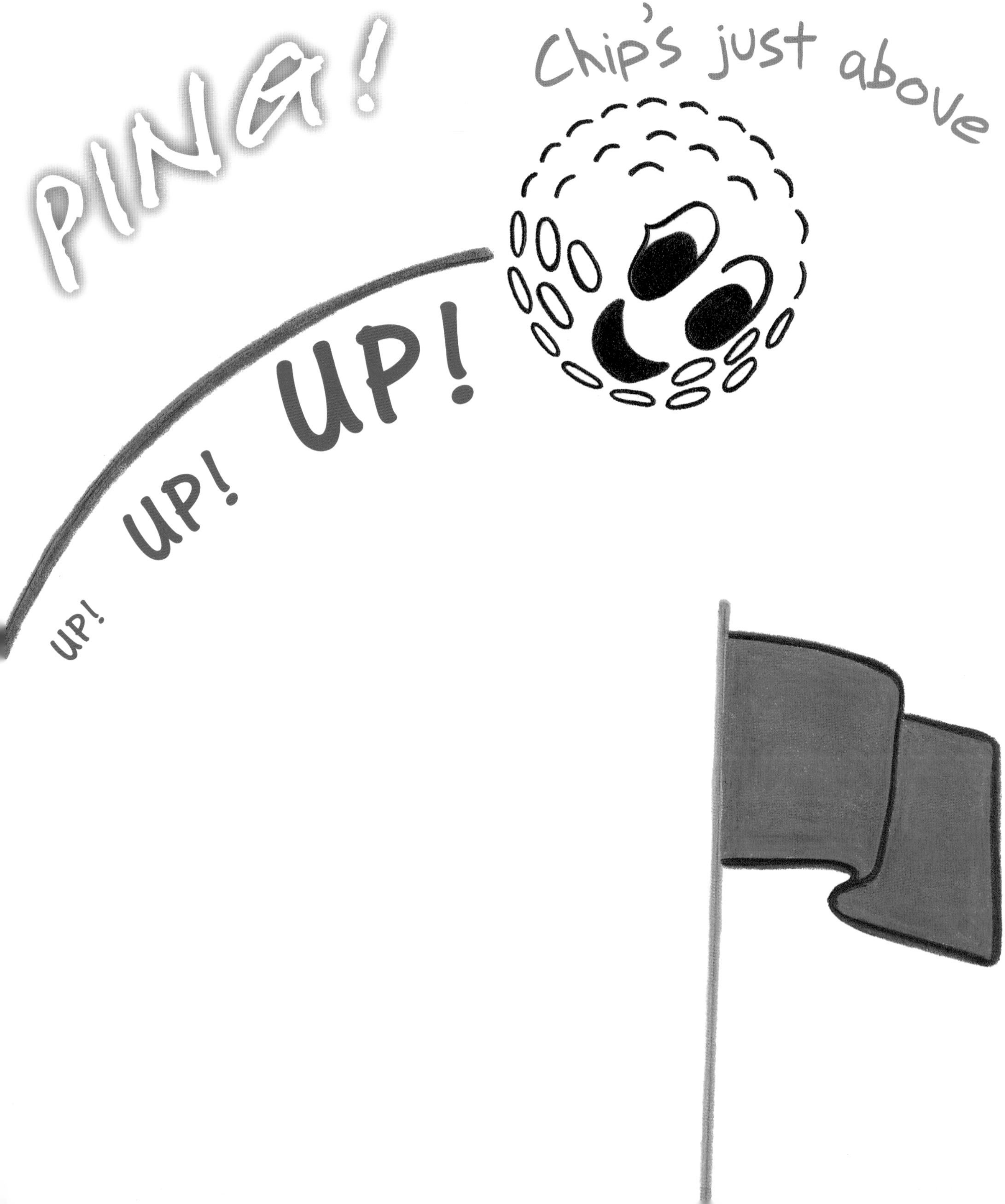

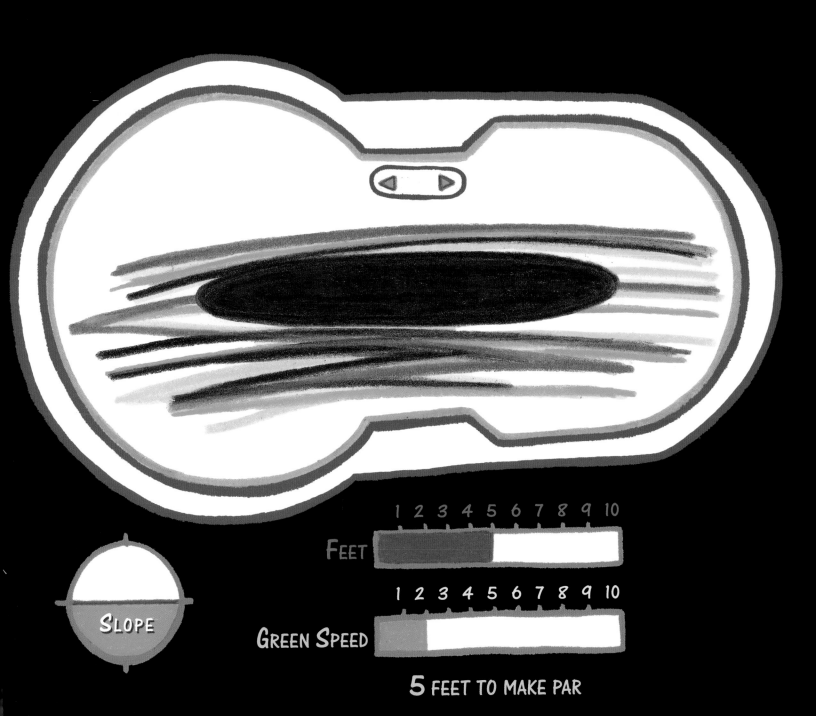

GOLF LINGO

CHIP– A short shot hit from near the green

COURSE– Playing area of 18 holes, each
with a tee box, fairway, and green

DIVOT– A chunk of turf removed while hitting a ball

DOGLEG– A bend in the fairway

DRIVE– The first shot off the tee

DRIVER– The furthest hitting club

FAIRWAY– Course area between the tee and the green

FORE– A warning shouted out if a ball could hit someone

FOURSOME– Four players playing together

FRINGE– Grass surrounding the green

GREEN– Short grass area for putting

HOLE– The round target in the green;
also one of 18 playing areas on a golf course